EXPLORER

THE MYSTERY BOXES

SEVEN GRAPHIC STORIES

EDITED BY KAZU KIBUISHI

AMULET BOOKS
NEW YORK

THANKS TO MY COEDITOR,
SHEILA KEENAN
—K.K.

Publisher's Note
This is a work of fiction. Names, characters, places, and incidents are either the product of the author's imagination or are used fictitiously, and any resemblances to actual person, living or dead, business establishments, events, or locales is entirely coincidental.

Cataloging-in-Publication Data has been applied for
and may be obtained from the Library of Congress.

Paperback ISBN 978-1-4197-0009-5
Hardcover ISBN 978-1-4197-0010-1

Book design by Chad W. Beckerman

Printed and bound in China
10 9 8 7 6 5

Amulet Books are available at special discounts when purchased in quantity for premiums and promotions as well as fundraising or educational use. For details, contact specialsales@abramsbooks.com, or the address below.

115 West 18th Street
New York, NY 10011
www.abramsbooks.com

CONTENTS

BY EMILY CARROLL

tap
tap
tap

I'm made of wax
and very small.
I'll be your friend,
not just a doll.
Keep me out of the sun
and we'll be fine.
What's mine is yours,
what's yours
is mine.

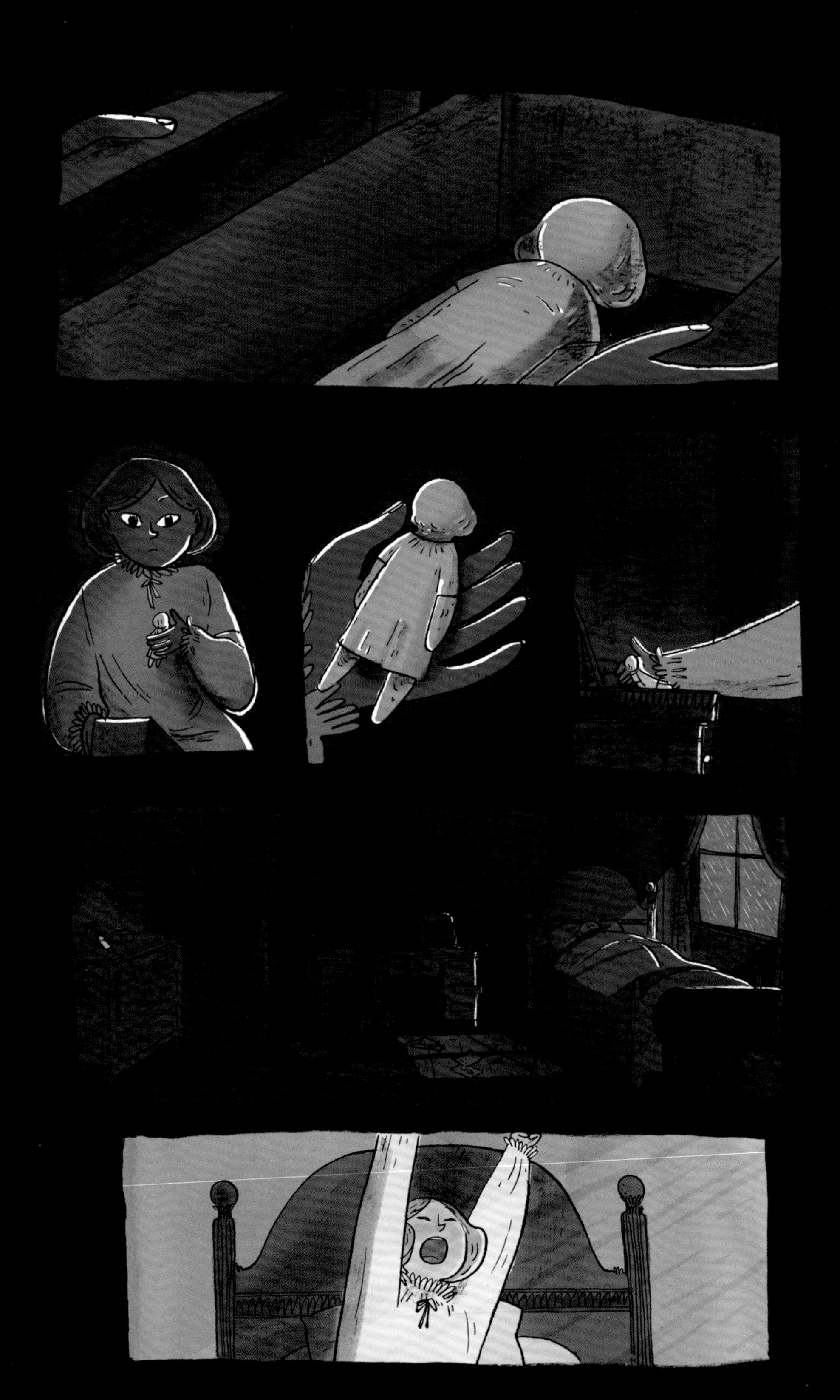

Don't forget your homework.
And that room of yours is an awful mess.
No going outside until you've tidied up!
...?

tap
tap
tap

Honey, you've been so good with your chores lately.
Why don't you take a well-deserved break?

Don't forget to do the sweeping!

Where do you think you're going?
Just what is this?
This is not how we do our schoolwork.
Try again.

GET IN HERE RIGHT NOW, YOUNG LADY!!!

Clean this up.
And go straight back to your room.

About last night, sweetheart...
I'm so sorry I yelled...
You've been so quiet and well behaved all morning...
In fact, I'm going to bake you a batch of cookies.

Clean up all the mud you tracked in!
What? I just gave you cookies a minute ago!
Go to sleep! I can hear you running around up there!
Who broke all my good dishes?
STOP!

RIGHT NOW.
And go away.
never.

Don't even think about going outside until these dishes are cleaned up!
clik

tap tap tap
tap tap tap
THUMP THUMP THUMP
THUMP THUMP THUMP
THUD THUD THUD
tap tap tap

Well, I hope you have a plan for cleaning all that up, too.
Of course.
I've got just the box to put it in.

Spring Cleaning
BY DAVE ROMAN
& RAINA TELGEMEIER

OLIVER, YOU HAVEN'T PLAYED WITH MOST OF THESE TOYS SINCE KINDERGARTEN!
BUT **DAD!**
oliver's Room KEEP OUT!
NO "BUTS." I WANT THIS CLOSET CLEANED OUT BY TOMORROW.

Y'KNOW, BRO, YOU COULD SELL SOME OF THIS STUFF ON eBUY!
I BET YOU COULD MAKE ENOUGH MONEY TO AFFORD SOME NEW VIDEO GAMES! LIKE SKULLTHUMPER II.
YOU'RE THE ONE WHO WANTS THAT GAME...
CLEAN OUT YOUR OWN CLOSET.
?

HEY, ROLAND? DO YOU RECOGNIZE THIS PUZZLE BOX?
NEVER SEEN IT.
SELL IT.
Blip Beep
FLASH
UPLOAD
CLICK
DING
DONG

THE BOX! PANT PANT
IS IT STILL FOR SALE?
HOW DID YOU GET HERE SO QUICK? I DIDN'T EVEN PUT AN ADDRESS IN MY POST.
UH...I'VE GOT A SPECIAL APP ON MY PHONE? ANYWAY, I'M WILLING TO PAY ONE HUNDRED DOLLARS FOR THAT BOX.
The Orzos
A HUNDRED DOLLARS?
YES! IN REAL MONEY!
I CAN DOUBLE WHATEVER THIS GUY IS OFFERING!!!

SHOVE
SLAM
SO DO WE HAVE A DEAL?
I DON'T KNOW IF–
MADAM! THERE IS NO NEED TO BE RUDE. I HAVE AS MUCH RIGHT TO DO BUSINESS HERE AS **ANY** WIZARD!
WIZARD?!
NOW, SIR. I'M SURE WE CAN COME TO AN **AGREEABLE ARRANGEMENT** IF YOU'LL GIVE ME A BALLPARK FIGURE.
WHAT DOES THE BOX EVEN DO?!
I'VE GOT TWO HUNDRED... DO I HEAR THREE?

WHOOSH
WIZARDS THESE DAYS! RESORTING TO USING MONEY. HAVE YOU NO PRIDE?!
MY GOOD LAD, I'M PREPARED TO OFFER YOU ANY WISH YOUR HEART MIGHT DESIRE! PERHAPS A PET UNICORN?
DOES HE LOOK LIKE THE TYPE OF KID WHO WANTS A UNICORN?
I CAN MAKE YOU TALLER. AND GIVE YOU BAT WINGS! BOYS LOVE BAT WINGS.
THAT'S ENOUGH.
ZAP!
RIBBIT!

UM, MAYBE WE COULD ALL... EXCUSE ME? **HELLO?**
?
Hide me, Oliver! These wizards are NUTS!

PSST! HEY, OLIVER!
OH. HI, VALERIE.
WHATCHA GOT THERE?
I'LL TELL YOU... IN YOUR HOUSE, OKAY?
SURE.

MIND IF I TAKE A CLOSER LOOK?
I'M NOT SURE IF...
YOU CAN **TRUST** ME. I'M AN EXPERT AT THESE TYPES OF THINGS.
MY PARENTS THINK I'M CRAZY, BUT I PLAN TO MAJOR IN ADVANCED MYSTICAL RESEARCH WHEN I GO TO COLLEGE.
?
HOW DID THOSE WIZARDS FIND ME?
YOU CAN'T PUT MAGICAL OBJECTS ON THE INTERNET WITHOUT STUFF LIKE THIS HAPPENING.
A LOT OF WIZARDS TROLL AROUND, WAITING FOR LOST ARTIFACTS TO REVEAL THEMSELVES.
Typey
Type
Type
MY GUESS IS THAT YOUR BOX IS ONE OF THESE.
Ancient Transport
Instant Death
"ENCHANTED WITH LIVING MAGIC, SORCERERS USE THEM TO CROSS INTO VARIOUS DIMENSIONS."

A BOX ONLY WORKS WITH ITS PARTNER. SUPPOSEDLY, THESE MATCHING SETS WERE ALL SCATTERED AND LOST DURING SOME WIZARD WAR BACK IN THE DAY.
POOR THING. ALL THESE YEARS, TRAPPED IN OUR WORLD.
ALL HE WANTS IS A SAFE PLACE TO REST.
THAT MUST BE WHY HE CHOSE YOUR MESSY CLOSET. PROBABLY THOUGHT YOU'D NEVER NOTICE WITH ALL YOUR OTHER JUNK.
IT'S A **GIRL**.
HOW CAN YOU TELL?
I HEARD HER VOICE IN MY **HEAD**.
SHE KNOWS MY NAME!

SHE'S TIRED OF CRAZY WIZARD SHENANIGANS. YOU THINK SHE CAN HIDE OUT HERE?
MY HOUSE IS TOO CLOSE TO YOURS. THEY'LL CHECK HERE EVENTUALLY.
AND AS MUCH AS I LOVE MAGIC, MY PARENTS WOULD KILL ME.
WHAT IF WE DIG A REALLY DEEP HOLE SOMEWHERE...OR HIDE HER AT THE BOTTOM OF THE OCEAN?
"LIVING MAGIC" MEANS IT'S **ALIVE**—SHE COULD SUFFOCATE OR DROWN. PLUS, I READ THESE BOXES GET LONELY BEING ONLY HALF A PAIR. THEY LIKE TO BE AROUND OTHER **STUFF**.
WHAT ABOUT A MUSEUM? OR AN ANTIQUES STORE?
I KNOW!

CORN FLAKES
silver polish
HI, AUNT ELLEN.

WE'RE GONNA GO DOWNSTAIRS AND PLAY SOME SKEE-BALL.
WHO'S YOUR FRIEND? SHE'S PRETTY.
MAKE SURE SHE DOESN'T TRIP OVER MY PORCELAIN PORPOISES!
WHEN YOU SAID YOUR AUNT WAS A PACK RAT, YOU WERE **NOT** KIDDING.
SKEE BALL
WHERE SHOULD WE HIDE YOU?
CRASH!

IT'S NO USE TRYING TO HIDE THE BOX! I HAPPEN TO BE A DETECTIVE AS WELL AS A WIZARD!
HURRY!
LOOK OVER THERE!
I THINK THEY RECOGNIZE EACH OTHER!
THIS VASE...
IT'S ANOTHER BOX!
POP!
!!!

My love! I'd lost hope of ever finding you again!
Thank you, Oliver and Valerie! Thank you both!
VOOOSH
POOF!
WHAT JUST HAPPENED?
THEY COMBINED POWERS TO MOVE TO ANOTHER DIMENSION WHERE THEY CAN HIDE TOGETHER?
JUST A THEORY.
THUMP
HMPH! CHILDREN, DO YOU KNOW THESE CHARACTERS?
NOT INTENTIONALLY.

MADAM! I AM WILLING TO OFFER YOU $5,000 FOR THIS ENTIRE LOT OF GOODS!
YOU'RE TOO LATE. THE BOX IS LONG GONE.
$10,000! WHAT DO YOU SAY? YOU COULD BUY TWICE AS MUCH JUNK...ER, BEAUTIFUL ANTIQUES, WITH THAT!
ARE YOU KIDDING? THIS PAINTING ALONE IS WORTH $10,000!
MINE!
I SAW IT FIRST!
THE END!

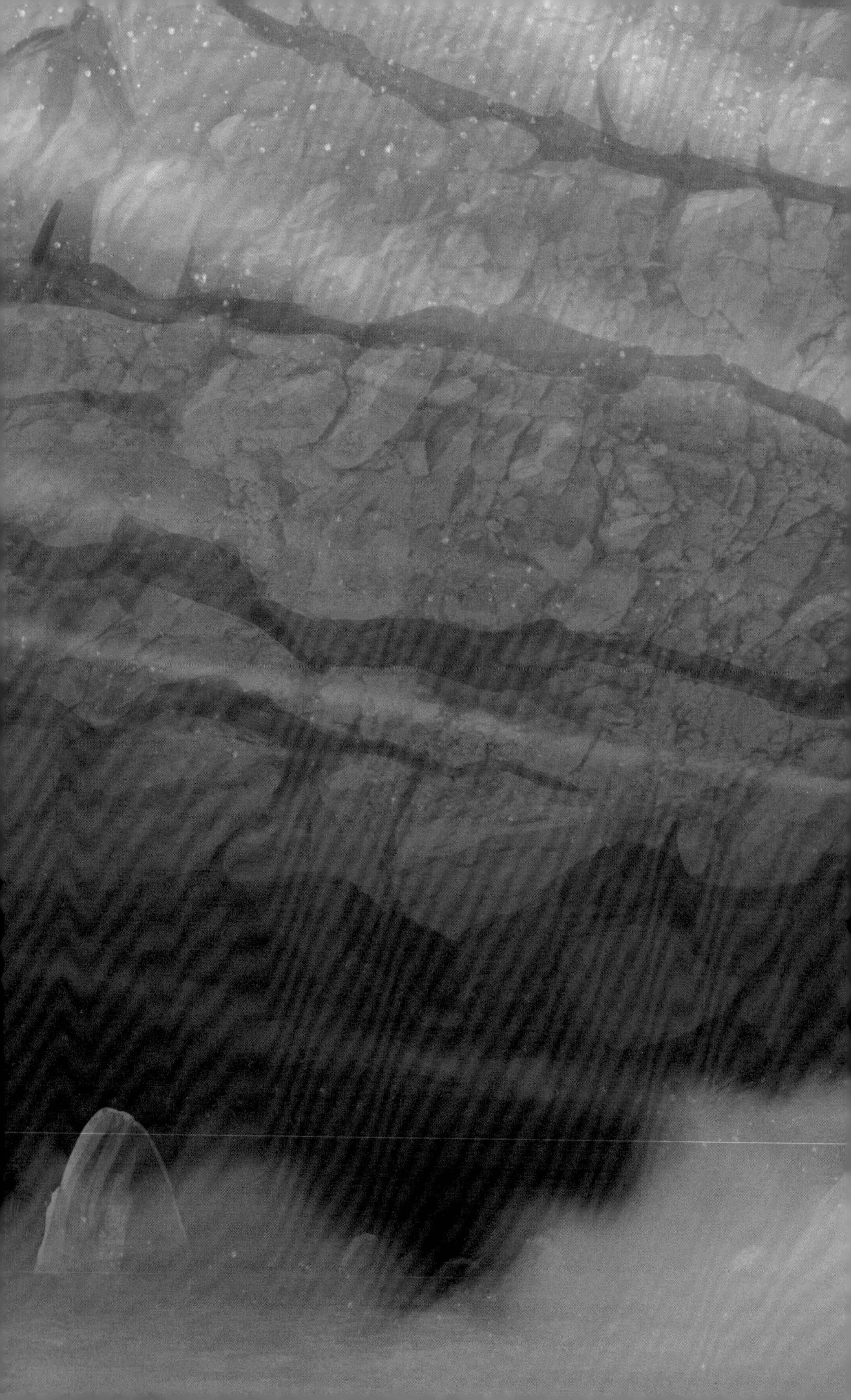

BY JASON CAFFOE

SIGH...
I CAN'T BELIEVE THIS.
TREASURE HERE
OF COURSE THIS STUPID PLACE ISN'T ON THE MAP.
WHY WOULD IT BE?

THE DINOSAURS WEREN'T ON THE MAP EITHER.
A LITTLE WARNING ABOUT THEM WOULD HAVE BEEN NICE.
AND MAYBE A HEADS-UP ABOUT THAT REVOLTING, ENDLESS BOG.
AND THE GLACIAL WASTELAND OUTSIDE OF NIGHTMARE VALE.

AND THEN, AFTER ALL THAT, I FINALLY REACH THIS TEMPLE,
AND I THINK MY TROUBLES ARE OVER!
TREASURE HERE
OH WAIT, THERE'S AN ENDLESS, EMPTY LABYRINTH INSIDE.
MIGHT'VE BEEN NICE TO HAVE SEEN THAT ON THE MAP, TOO.

NOW EVEN IF I MANAGE TO REACH THE TREASURE, I DOUBT I CAN FIND MY WAY OUT OF...
...HERE...

NO, NO, NO, NO, NO!

TRIP!
OOF!
FWIP!
PLINK!
AGH!

EESH!
WHAT'S THE BIG IDEA?!
CAN'T A GUY EVEN SAY HELLO AROUND HERE?
...UM... H-HELLO?
HI THERE! NICE TO MEET YOU!
WHAT BRINGS YOU ALL THE WAY OUT HERE?
UM... I'M LOOKING FOR A... TREASURE CHEST?

A WHAT?
IT'S... LIKE A SPECIAL KIND OF BOX...
OH, THAT!
JUST FOLLOW ME!
YOU KNOW, IT'S BEEN A LONG TIME SINCE I'VE SPOKEN TO ANYONE.
NOT A LOT OF PEOPLE MAKE IT OUT TO THIS TEMPLE,
AND THE ONES THAT DO USUALLY DON'T FIND ME.
I FIND THEM.

HOW LONG HAVE YOU BEEN HERE?
MY WHOLE LIFE.
I'VE WATCHED OVER THIS LABYRINTH FOR AS LONG AS I CAN REMEMBER.
AH, HERE WE ARE!
STAND BACK, PLEASE.
FWEE!

BKOOM!
THAT WAS AMAZING!
THANK YOU!
IS THIS WHAT YOU WERE LOOKING FOR?
IT'S BEAUTIFUL...

WHAT'S IN IT?
I ACTUALLY DON'T KNOW,
BUT IT'S MY FAVORITE THING IN THE TEMPLE.
HAVEN'T YOU EVER WONDERED WHAT'S INSIDE?
OF COURSE!
IT COULD BE FULL OF ANCIENT ARTIFACTS,
LONG-LOST REMNANTS OF AN ANCIENT EXPEDITION.
OR THERE COULD BE A DRAGON EGG INSIDE,
THOUSANDS OF YEARS OLD, BUT STILL HOT TO THE TOUCH,

JUST WAITING TO HATCH INTO A FEROCIOUS BEAST!
OR MAYBE THERE'S A GENIE INSIDE!
AN ALL-POWERFUL BEING,
ABLE TO GRANT ANY WISH OUR HEARTS DESIRE!
THOUGH THE BOX COULD ALSO BE CURSED...
AND OPENING IT COULD UNLEASH A PLAGUE THAT WOULD WASH OVER EVEN THE MOST DISTANT LANDS,
CONSUMING EVERYTHING IN ITS PATH.

OR PERHAPS THERE'S A WHOLE OTHER WORLD INSIDE, JUST LIKE OURS, WITH LITTLE PEOPLE, JUST LIKE US, LOOKING AT A BOX JUST LIKE THIS ONE AND WONDERING...
IT'S GOLD!
HM?
IT'S FULL OF GOLD! PURE GOLD!
OH. HOW INTERESTING.
THIS IS GREAT!
YES, GREAT.

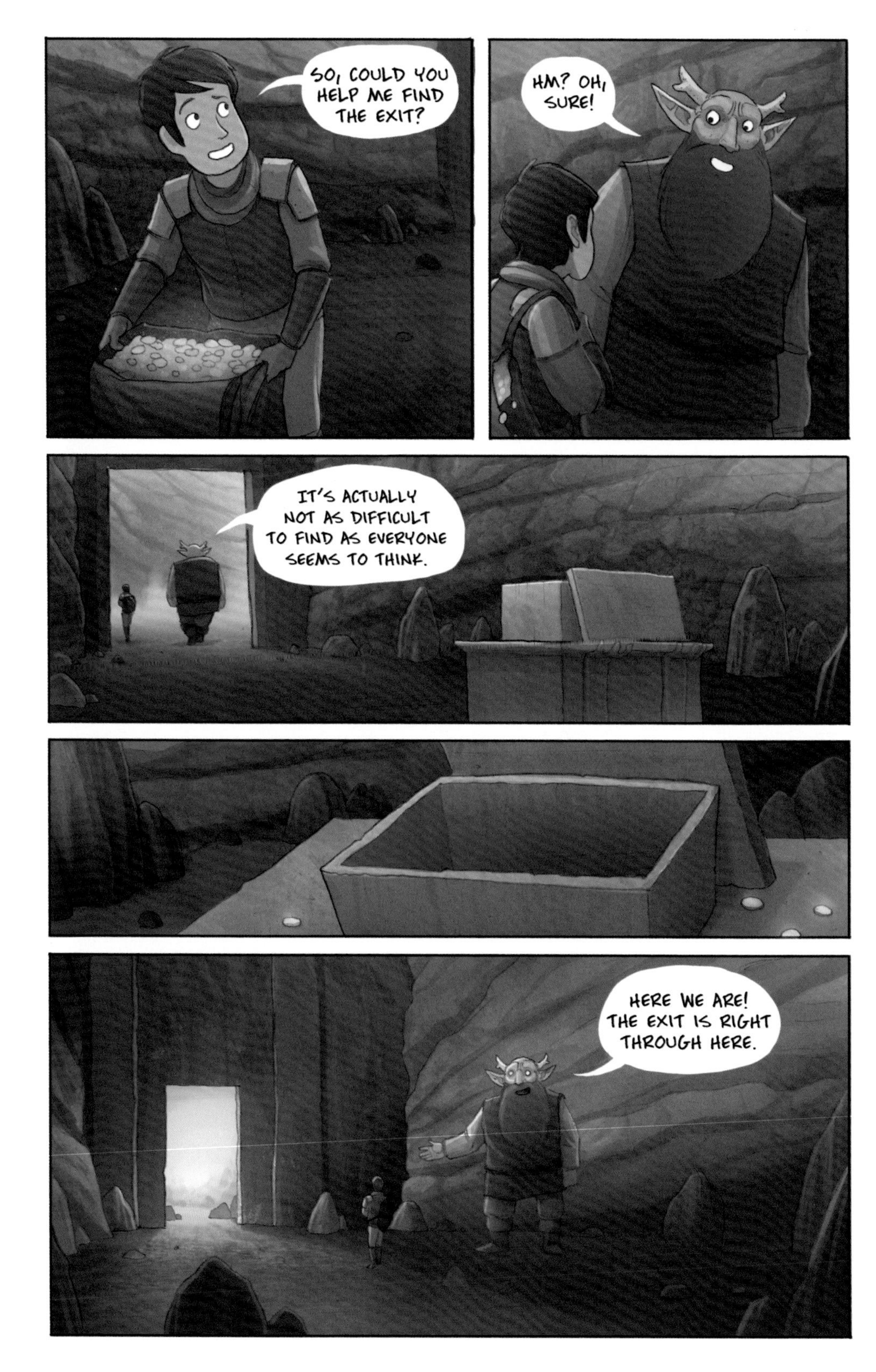
SO, COULD YOU HELP ME FIND THE EXIT?
HM? OH, SURE!
IT'S ACTUALLY NOT AS DIFFICULT TO FIND AS EVERYONE SEEMS TO THINK.
HERE WE ARE! THE EXIT IS RIGHT THROUGH HERE.

YOU KNOW, YOU SHOULD COME WITH ME!
I COULD REALLY USE SOMEONE LIKE YOU, AND YOU'D BE ABLE TO SEE THE WORLD!
OH, NO THANK YOU.
I'VE SPENT SO MUCH TIME IMAGINING WHAT THINGS ARE LIKE OUTSIDE THESE WALLS, THERE'S JUST NO WAY IT COULD LIVE UP TO MY EXPECTATIONS.
AND EVEN IF IT DID, SOMEONE NEEDS TO LOOK AFTER THIS PLACE.
HM.
WELL, THANKS FOR YOUR HELP!
OF COURSE! GOOD LUCK ON YOUR TRAVELS!

POOR GUY...
HE DOESN'T KNOW WHAT HE'S MISSING.

-END-

BY RAD SECHRIST

この乳酪を盗みたる者
MOM...
呪われ
WHAT'S GRANDMA DOING?
竹箱の中に
SIGH... SHE THINKS THERE'S A SPIRIT STEALING BUTTER FROM THE FRIDGE...
永遠に
AND SHE'S TRYING TO TRAP IT.
OBAASAN! THERE IS NO SPIRIT...
閉じ込むるべし!!
STEALING BUTTER—
SNAP!

あっ
SHE SAYS SHE CAUGHT IT.
捕えたかのう

WHO DARES...
TO TRAP MELPHADOR?

ZIMAPOTHS!
ZAP!
POOF!
HEY, WHAT DID YOU DO TO ME?
THAT'S WHAT YOU GET, HUMAN.
CONSIDER IT AN IMPROVEMENT!
BARK!
GASP!
NO!

NO! THE THUSELA!
WHY?!!
CURSE YOU, BEAST!
I ALMOST HAD ENOUGH! I WAS SO CLOSE!
WHAT AM I GOING TO DO?
I CAN GET MORE! MORE THUSELA!
NO, WAIT! I CAN'T! THE OLD WRINKLY ONE IS TOO DANGEROUS!
I'LL GET YOU MORE... THUSELA...
IF YOU TURN ME BACK.

FINE, BUT FIRST WE BETTER REST.
IT'S A FAR JOURNEY TO THE KITCHEN.
A FAR JOURNEY?
HI.
HELLO...
HEY! DON'T TOUCH THOSE!
DON'T YOU KNOW ANYTHING ABOUT THE SPIRIT WORLD? THOSE THINGS ARE DANGEROUS!
LETS JUST HOPE THEY DON'T FOLLOW US NOW.
THEY'RE BAD LUCK SPIRITS.
BUT, THEY'RE SO CUTE...

HE'S A PROTECTIVE SPIRIT. HE GUARDS YOUR HOUSE FROM BAD OR DISHONEST SPIRITS.

SO, THIS IS HOW YOU GET IN THE HOUSE.
C'MON! TO THE THUSELA.
IS THIS ONE DANGEROUS?
OF COURSE NOT. HE WOULDN'T HAVE GOTTEN PAST THE GUARDIAN SPIRIT IF HE WAS.
OH...
PAT PAT
THEN, HOW DID YOU GET PAST THE GUARDIAN SPIRIT?
HA-HA! VERY FUNNY, HUMAN.
OK. WE'RE HERE. THE THUSELA IS PAST THE PILLARS OF DOOM!

BEWARE THE OLD WRINKLY ONE.
PAST THE PILLARS OF DOOM!
THE THUSELA.

GASP!
CREAK
...
GASP!

SLICE!
OH NO!
PHEW.
WHAP!
SLAM!

GHAAAH!
I GOT IT, MELPHADOR!
YES, YES! THROW IT HERE!
WHAP!

OH!

GRANDMA! WAIT, IT'S ME!

SQUEAK SQUEAK SQUEAK

YOU FAILED! ENJOY BEING A SPIRIT.
THUSELA!
WAIT, MELPHADOR! I GOT SOME!

THUSELA! YOU HAVE TO TURN ME BACK!
WHAT AM I GOING TO DO WITH THAT?
WELL, I GUESS YOU DON'T HAVE TO HONOR OUR DEAL...
I MEAN, IF YOU WANT TO BE...
A DISHONEST SPIRIT.
HA-HA, OF COURSE I WAS ONLY KIDDING!
I'LL CHANGE YOU RIGHT BACK!

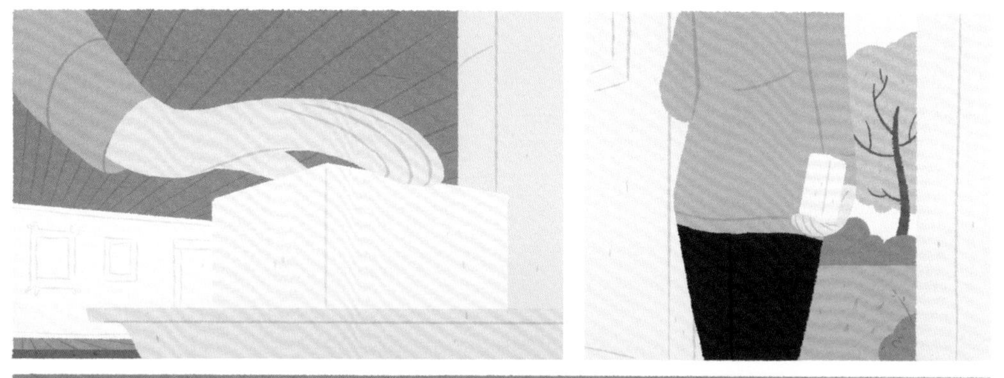

The Soldier's Daughter

BY STUART LIVINGSTON

WITH STEPHANIE RAMIREZ

FOR MY BROTHER AND ME, THE WAR MEANT ONE THING: WAITING.
WAITING FOR NEWS OF OUR FATHER... WAITING FOR THE WAR TO END.
ALWAYS WAITING.
THEN A LETTER ARRIVED.
FATHER WAS DEAD.
KILLED IN BATTLE BY A VICIOUS ENEMY...
THAT WICKED DOG...
CAPTAIN VAAL!

DON'T FOLLOW ME, JACK.
I HAVE TO DO THIS.
DO WHAT, CLARA? AND WHY ARE YOU TAKING FATHER'S THINGS?
I'M GOING TO FIND THE MAN WHO KILLED HIM.
SHH...
CAPTAIN...
VAAL.
YOU CAN'T BE SERIOUS!

JUST WHAT DO YOU THINK HUNTING HIM DOWN WILL ACCOMPLISH?
I'VE ALREADY ONE GRAVE TO DIG. I WON'T DIG A SECOND!
SHAK!
LOOK AT YOURSELF, CLARA.
YOU CAN'T STOP ME, JACK.
YOU HOLD A SWORD TO YOUR OWN BROTHER?
IS REVENGE WORTH THIS?
I WON'T LET FATHER'S DEATH BE IN VAIN.
HE WOULD HAVE WANTED THIS.
HE WOULD HAVE WANTED US TO STAY TOGETHER, HERE, AT HOME, WHERE IT'S SAFE!

FATHER GAVE EVERYTHING...
HIS LIFE...TO PROTECT US AND OUR KINGDOM.
IMAGINE HIS SHAME...
IF HE KNEW HE'D RAISED A COMPLETE...
COWARD OF A SON!
SLAM!
I'LL FIND THE DARK CAPTAIN, FATHER.
I'LL MAKE HIM PAY!

THE WESTERN FRONT.
BOOM
KRAK
KRAK...
BRMM...
WAR RAGES.
I'M ALMOST THERE, FATHER.
EEEEEEEEEEEEEEE
BOOM!
ALMOST THERE.
KRSH!
KRSH!

KRAK... BANG... BANG...
O-OW...
THAT WAS QUITE A CLOSE CALL.
COME NOW, CHILD. WE MUST HURRY.
THANK YOU, SIR.
I APPRECIATE THE—OOH—HELP.
...
YES, WELL... I MUST BE GOING.
YOU WERE RIGHT ABOUT HER.
SHE IS BRASH, FULL OF ANGER...AND IMPULSIVE ABOVE ALL ELSE.
!

CAN I SAVE THIS ONE TOO?
WAR IS A DARK POWER, CLARA.
MANY WHO RIDE IN BATTLE WILL FIND THIS POWER—MANY MORE WILL BE CONSUMED BY IT. NOT EVERYONE HAS THE STRENGTH TO RESIST.
CAPTAIN VAAL, FOR ONE...
WH-WHAT DID YOU SAY?
FWOOM!
AND YOUR FATHER...
SHK!
WHO ARE YOU? A SPY?!
NO...A MESSENGER.
WITH AN URGENT DELIVERY.
WHAT...
WHAT IS THIS?

DO YOU TRULY SEEK VENGEANCE FOR YOUR FATHER? CAN YOU REALLY FACE THE FORMIDABLE CAPTAIN VAAL? ARE YOU STRONG...**ENOUGH?**
THIS BOX MAY HOLD THE ANSWERS...WILL YOU LOOK?
KCHK!
CAN YOU OVERCOME THE DARK POWER OF WAR?
OR WILL IT CONSUME YOU AS WELL?

...
...
...
SSH...
SSH...
FSSH...
SSH...
SO... HE FOUND YOU AFTER ALL.
FATHER...?
IS IT... IS IT REALLY YOU?

YES, DEAR.
I'M HERE.
I...
I NEVER THOUGHT I'D SEE YOU AGAIN.
WHAT IS THIS PLACE?
WHO ARE THESE PEOPLE?

WHY ARE WE HERE, FATHER?
I'M AFRAID THIS IS MY DOING.
I KNOW WHAT YOU INTEND TO DO. AND I CAN'T LET THAT HAPPEN.
CLARA.
DON'T LET YOUR ANGER DESTROY YOU...AS I DID.
IN THE THICK OF BATTLE, AS MY SWORD CLANGED AND STRUCK HOME...
A GREAT DARKNESS GREW WITHIN ME.
I TRIED TO FIGHT IT, WITH THOUGHTS OF YOU...
AND JACK...
BUT IT WAS TOO LATE.

MY RAGE AND ANGER GREW. MY HATRED SET MY COURSE... TOWARD CAPTAIN VAAL.
I PAID FOR THIS DARKNESS WITH MY LIFE.
AND THESE PEOPLE, TOO, ARE...
WE AWAIT ARRIVAL OF A SHIP TO TAKE US ON OUR FINAL VOYAGE.
WARRIORS, ALL.
BUT FATHER. YOU WERE WRONGED!
AND I WILL MAKE CAPTAIN VAAL PAY FOR HIS CRIMES.
AFTER WHAT HE DID...
NO, CLARA.
THERE'S NOTHING MORE YOU CAN DO FOR ME, BUT THIS...
BE AT PEACE.
LET GO OF YOUR ANGER.
WAR TAKES NO SIDES...
AND SPARES NO SIDES...

CAPTAIN...
VAAL.
YOU, ALL OF OUR PEOPLE, MUST LET GO OF HATRED, CLARA.
DON'T LET THIS VIOLENCE CONTINUE ANY LONGER.
IT'S TIME.
GOOD-BYE, MY DEAREST DAUGHTER.
BUT...YOU CAN'T GO!
I NEED YOU, FATHER.
YOU'RE STRONG, CLARA.
BUT YOU MUST DIRECT THAT STRENGTH.
TAKE CARE OF JACK.
YOU ONLY HAVE EACH OTHER NOW.
...
YES, FATHER.

I'LL DO MY BEST.
I'M SORRY, YOUNG ONE.
THIS MUST HAVE BEEN DIFFICULT FOR YOU.
NO... IT'S OKAY.
I KNOW NOW WHAT I MUST DO.
WAIT!
PLEASE, TELL ME... WHO ARE YOU?
JUST A MESSENGER.

NOTHING MORE.
CLARA?!
YOU'RE... BACK.
...
JACK...

OH, JACK. YOU WERE RIGHT. VENGEANCE, ALL THIS KILLING, IS NOT THE ANSWER.
WE MUST DO SOMETHING TO END THIS WAR.
CLARA...
AND FORGIVE ME FOR THE CRUEL THINGS I SAID LAST NIGHT.
I'M JUST GLAD YOU'RE SAFE.
COME ON INSIDE. YOU MUST BE STARVING.
YES. IT HAS BEEN A LONG NIGHT.
END.

Whatzit
BY JOHANE MATTE
WITH SAYMONE PHANEKHAM

THIS IS ONE OF THE BIGGEST CONTRACTS OUR COMPANY HAS EVER UNDERTAKEN.

WE WILL BE SHIPPING THE REPLICA OF A COMPLETE SOLAR SYSTEM FOR THE GRAND UNIVERSAL EXHIBITION.
ALL CREWS MUST WORK TOGETHER TO ACHIEVE THIS!
THERE'S A LOT TO DO, AND I KNOW WE'RE SHORT ON PERSONNEL AND ON TIME.
SINCE WE'LL NEED EVERY BIT OF HELP, I'VE PROMOTED MY GRANDSON TO CHECKLIST DUTY.
PFF.
I BELIEVE HE'LL DO A GOOD JOB.
PAT! PAT!
READY FOR WORK, DEET?
YES, GRAMPA!
TEACHER'S PET...

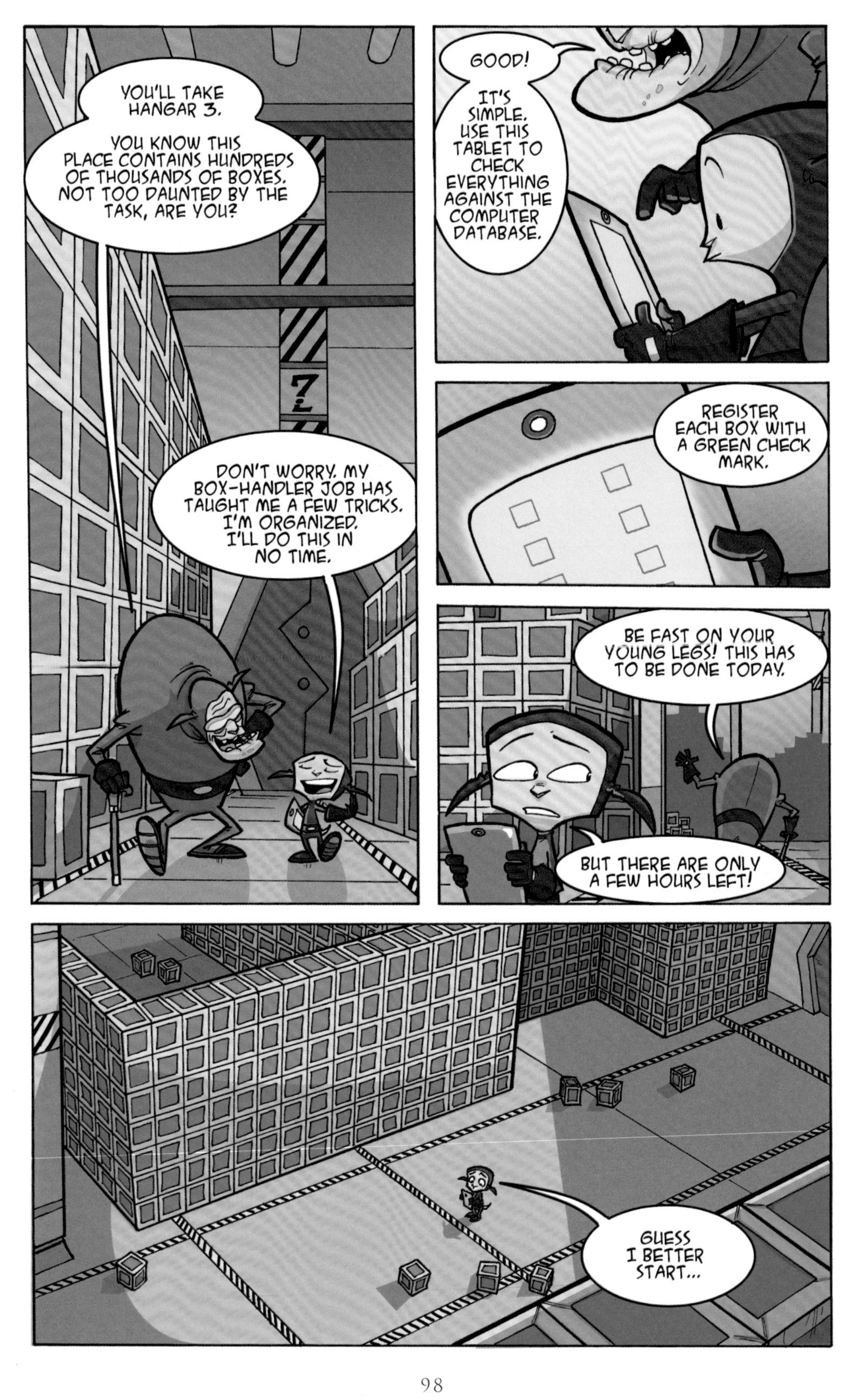
YOU'LL TAKE HANGAR 3.
YOU KNOW THIS PLACE CONTAINS HUNDREDS OF THOUSANDS OF BOXES. NOT TOO DAUNTED BY THE TASK, ARE YOU?
DON'T WORRY. MY BOX-HANDLER JOB HAS TAUGHT ME A FEW TRICKS. I'M ORGANIZED. I'LL DO THIS IN NO TIME.
GOOD!
IT'S SIMPLE. USE THIS TABLET TO CHECK EVERYTHING AGAINST THE COMPUTER DATABASE.
REGISTER EACH BOX WITH A GREEN CHECK MARK.
BE FAST ON YOUR YOUNG LEGS! THIS HAS TO BE DONE TODAY.
BUT THERE ARE ONLY A FEW HOURS LEFT!
GUESS I BETTER START...

KER-FLASH!
KER-FLASH!
KER-FLASH!
KER-FLASH!
KER-FLASH!
KER-FLASH!
KER-FLASH!

KER-FLASH!
No Database Match.
ERRRRT!
SET: Content Search.
BOOP!
KER-FLASH!
WARGL!
Still No Database Match.
SCRATCH! SCRATCH!

WARGL!
WHAT THE...? GET BACK IN YOUR BOX!!
NURGL!
CRUMBLE
OH NO.
NO,
NO,
NO,
NO, NO, NO!!

GAH!
IT RUINED THE ZOOLOGICAL SECTOR!
FIRST I BETTER CATCH THESE CRITTERS, THEN...
BOWLING BALLS?
I'VE GOT A BAD FEELING ABOUT THIS.
OH, NO...
NOT PLANETS!!

MUST STOP COSMIC PINBALL!
DIDN'T CATCH THEM ALL.
ROLL!
CRASH!
EEP!

NAGL?
YOU! GET OVER—
DEET?
JUST CHECKING IN.
IS ALL GOING WELL?
OHYESGRAMPAABSOLUTELY EVERYTHINGISGOINGSMOOTHLY TIPTOPSHAPENOWORRIES!!
GOOD! I'LL DROP BY FOR A SHORT VISIT LATER.
UH-OH.
I HAVE TO QUICKLY CLEAN ALL THIS
BUT I BETTER CAPTURE THAT THING FIRST OR IT WILL KEEP MESSING EVERYTHING UP!
HMMM...

GL?
HAGL! HAGL! HAGL! HAGL!
HA!
GOTCHA!
WHOMP!
GOTTA HURRY, GOTTA HURRY!
SCRAPE!
SCRAPE!
SCRAPE!
SCRAPE!
FWOOOM!

LAST ONE!
Kwiiiiiii...
DEET? A WORD?
EEP!
...iiK!

I DON'T KNOW HOW THE WHATZIT ENDED UP IN YOUR HANGAR.
UNIVERSAL
NARGL!
IT DEFINITELY DIDN'T BELONG IN THAT SOLAR SYSTEM.
BOXES
MISPLACED BOXES ARE A COMMON PROBLEM, DEET.
UNIVERSAL
BOXES
UNFORTUNATELY, YOU WERE NOT PREPARED TO HANDLE THE SITUATION...
PERHAPS I WAS HASTY IN PROMOTING YOU.
I'LL RETURN YOU TO YOUR OLD POST.
I'M SURE YOU'LL BE READY FOR THIS JOB IN A FEW MORE YEARS.
SIGH!

POOR GRAMPA. I'VE RUINED HIS DAY.
I BETTER ASK THESE GUYS WHERE THIS BOX GOES. I DON'T WANT TO MESS UP AGAIN...
HA HA HA
DON'T YOU THINK USING THE WHATZIT WAS A BIT CRUEL FOR A PRANK?
NAH, THE KID DESERVED IT!
EASY FOR YOU TO SAY! I HAVE TO DEAL WITH ALL THOSE BROKEN BOXES.
HE THOUGHT HE COULD JUMP RANK EASY WITH HELP FROM HIS GRAMPA...
BUT HIS JUMP WAS MORE LIKE A TUMBLE!
AHAHA HAHAHAHAHAHAHA

SEE YOU GUYS LATER!
I GOT ME SOME INSPECTING TO DO!
?!
WHAT HAVE WE HERE?
GEMS?
PRETTY POOR PACKING JOB.
BETTER CHECK THE CONTENTS, MAKE SURE NOTHING HAS BEEN TAMPERED WITH... YET! HEH! HEH! HEH!
FRZZT!
WAAAAAAAAAAAA
HAGL!
♫
THE END.

The Escape Option

By Kazu Kibuishi

WHOA.

COME ON.
COME ON.
RUMMAGE!
WHIRRRRR
FOOMP!!
BLORP!

AAGH!

POP!
OOF!
WELCOME ABOARD, JAMES.

MAKE YOURSELF AT HOME.
HOW DO YOU KNOW MY NAME?
I KNOW EVERYTHING ABOUT YOU.
THAT'S WHY YOU'VE BEEN CHOSEN.
I WANT TO GIVE YOU THE CHANCE TO ESCAPE FROM YOUR PLANET BEFORE IT IS TOO LATE.
ESCAPE?
YOU SHOULD CONSIDER YOURSELF VERY LUCKY.

I HAVE BEEN TRAVELING ACROSS THE UNIVERSE COLLECTING SAMPLES OF LIFE FORMS ON THE VERGE OF EXTINCTION.
I HATE TO BE THE BEARER OF BAD NEWS,
BUT HUMANS ARE ABOUT TO GO BELLY UP.
IS OUR PLANET DYING?
EARTH HAS BEEN HERE FOR BILLIONS OF YEARS.
IT'S GOING TO BE FINE.
PERCY, SHOW HIM EARTH IN THE FUTURE.
How far into the future?
TWO THOUSAND YEARS.

Human technology, however, will not be advanced enough to transport them to the next planet capable of sustaining their occupancy.
If my data projections are correct, humans will need to find a new planet to colonize by this time.
It will only be a matter of time before all humans perish.
THERE HAS TO BE SOMETHING WE CAN DO!
THAT'S WHERE YOU COME IN.
PERCY, SHOW HIM THE CITY OF TESEN.
Show him the city in its glory days?
YES.
VRRR
RN

YOU WILL BE JOINING ME ON MY HOME PLANET, REQUIUS, WHERE YOU, ALONG WITH SEVERAL OTHERS, WILL PROUDLY REPRESENT THE HUMAN RACE.
YOUR KNOWLEDGE AND EXPERIENCE WILL BECOME AN INVALUABLE RESOURCE FOR THE PRESERVATION OF HUMANKIND.
WHY WAS I SELECTED TO BE A PART OF THIS?
OF ALL THE PEOPLE ON EARTH, WHY ME?

WE PROFILED MILLIONS OF CANDIDATES AND YOU EXHIBITED AN IDEAL MIXTURE OF INTELLIGENCE, EMPATHY, YOUTH, AND CURIOSITY.
EVEN AS A CHILD, YOU OFTEN DREAMED OF TRAVELING TO FAR AWAY WORLDS.
BUT NOT LIKE THIS.
NOT WHEN I KNOW WHAT'S GOING TO HAPPEN.
I CAN'T GO WITH YOU.
I HAVE TO STAY AND DO SOMETHING TO HELP.
YOU'RE GOING TO WALK AWAY FROM THIS OPPORTUNITY?
YES.

GOOD.
GOOD?
YOU'RE NOT UPSET?
IT'S YOUR CHOICE, MY FRIEND.
MY JOB IS TO TRAVEL ACROSS THE UNIVERSE AND PRESERVE LIFE.
TAP TAP
AND THERE'S MORE THAN ONE WAY TO ACCOMPLISH THAT.
GOOD LUCK, JAMES.

OH, NOT AGAIN.
WHIRRR
BLOOMP!
FSSH!
FOOMP!
SPLAT!

PSHEWW!

You didn't tell him the truth.
I TOLD HIM WHAT HE NEEDED TO HEAR.
You didn't tell him what happened to Requius.
HE DOESN'T NEED TO KNOW ABOUT OUR FAILURES.
IF JAMES IS GOING TO DO ANYTHING TO SAVE HIS PEOPLE, IT'S BETTER THAT HE DOESN'T ACT OUT OF FEAR.
And what if he had chosen differently?

THEN HE WOULD HAVE LEARNED THE TRUTH.
SOMETHING I FEEL HE ALREADY KNOWS...
THAT ESCAPE WAS NEVER AN OPTION.

ABOUT THE CREATORS

JASON CAFFOE is a graduate of the Savannah College of Art and Design and a contributor to the *Flight* anthologies. He works as the lead production assistant for Kazu Kibuishi, contributing colors and background art to the *Amulet* series. He also worked on Jake Parker's middle-school graphic novel *Missile Mouse*. Visit him at www.jasoncaffoe.com.

EMILY CARROLL is an up-and-coming artist who works in animation for children's television. She is a contributor to *The Anthology Project*, vol. 2, and her comics and art can also be found at www.emcarroll.com.

KAZU KIBUISHI is the creator of *Amulet*, the award-winning *New York Times*–bestselling middle-school graphic novel series. He was also the editor and art director of eight volumes of *Flight*, the groundbreaking, Eisner-nominated graphic anthology. His graphic collection *Copper* is a Junior Library Guild selection, and his earlier work *Daisy Kutter* was named a YALSA Best Book for Young Adults. For more on Kazu, check out www.boltcity.com.

STUART LIVINGSTON is an American Samoan comics and storyboard artist who lives in Los Angeles. He has contributed to both the *Flight* and *Popgun* anthologies and has produced storyboards for Disney, Warner Bros., Cartoon Network, and others. As a lifelong fan of Japanese RPGs, he was most heavily influenced by games like *Final Fantasy VI* and *Chrono Trigger* while making this comic. Visit him at www.stuartlivingston.com.

JOHANE MATTE has worked as a storyboard artist at Nickelodeon and is now at Dreamworks. Her film and television credits include *How to Train Your Dragon* and *Avatar: The Last Airbender*. Her comics work has appeared in several volumes of *Flight*.

DAVE ROMAN is the creator of *Astronaut Academy: Zero Gravity*. He is the coauthor of *The Last Airbender: Zuko's Story* and *X-Men: Misfits* (a *New York Times* bestseller) and also the creator of the teen horror graphic novel *Agnes Quill: An Anthology of Mystery*. Roman is a Harvey Award nominee and an Ignatz Award and Web Cartoonists' Choice Award winner. See more of his work at yaytime.com.

RAD SECHRIST is a cartoonist, a contributor to *Flight*, and a storyboard artist at Dreamworks, where he worked on *Kung Fu Panda II* and *Megamind*.

RAINA TELGEMEIER is the creator of the popular middle-school graphic novel *Smile*, which won a 2011 Eisner Award, a 2010 Boston Globe–Horn Book Award Honor, and a Children's Choice Book Award. She previously adapted and illustrated *The Baby-Sitters Club* into a series of graphic novels. Telgemeier's work has made the YALSA Great Graphic Novels for Teens, ALA Top 10 Graphic Novels for Youth, *Kirkus* Best Books, and ALA Notable Children's Books lists. See more of her work at goraina.com.

* * *

SAYMONE PHANEKHAM helped color "Whatzit." He lives in Montreal, Quebec.

STEPHANIE RAMIREZ helped write and color "The Soldier's Daughter." She lives in Los Angeles, where she works as an illustrator and character designer in animation.